THE *Winter*
BEACH PATROL

Story by
Rachel Griffiths
Illustrations by
Coral Tulloch

Jason loved living near the beach. Although summer was over, he still walked on the beach every day. He loved to watch the waves break on the rocks, and roll back in to the beach. At this time of year, the beach was deserted, apart from an occasional walker or fisherman, but there were plenty of seabirds. Jason always carried scraps of food in his pocket for the birds. He loved to watch the gulls squabbling over the scraps he threw along the shore, the terns diving for fish out beyond the breaking waves, and the pelicans wading in the shallows.

One windy afternoon on his way home from school, Jason noticed a long, black streak on the water. As he came closer, he could see dark stuff, like paint, covering the beach pebbles. He put his finger on it, and it came away black and sticky. "It's oil," he thought.

Close by, he saw a tern floundering on the sand. As he approached, he saw that its feathers were a glistening black from the oil.

Jason rushed to pick it up, but it pecked at him. Thinking fast, he slipped off his jacket and threw it over the bird. Then he wrapped it up and held it tight, so that just its beak and the tip of its head poked out.

He wondered what he should do next. Just then his friend, Joe, shouted to him, "Hey, Jason, what have you got there?"

"A tern. It was caught in the oil," Jason shouted back. "What should we do with it?"

"Let's take it to the environmental center. Don will know what to do."

They ran as fast as they could back along the beach, up the steps, past the bandstand, and over the boardwalk to the environmental center. As they entered, Don looked up. "What's happened? What do you have there?" he asked.

"We've found a tern," said Joe. "Jason found it on the beach."

"It's covered in oil and can't fly," said Jason, thrusting his bundle toward Don.

"Well, you've come to the right place," said Don. "Melanie, here, cares for injured birds, so she'll be able to look after it."

Melanie looked at Jason's bundle. "You've done the right thing by wrapping it up warmly. Birds try to clean the oil off their feathers with their beaks—that's called preening—and if they get too much inside their bodies, it kills them. Here we can clean them. This is the third bird we've seen today."

She took them into a large workroom with one whole wall lined with cages. Some of the cages held birds—two seagulls, a loon, and another tern. The rest were empty.

"These seagulls are ready to be released tomorrow," said Melanie. "The tern and the loon only came in this

morning, so they'll need at least two more days here. I hope I don't get too many more."

"Where has the oil come from?" asked Jason.

"I don't know," said Melanie. "We haven't been told of a major spill, so it's probably oil that has been spilled by a fishing boat. Four years ago, an oil tanker ran onto the reef, and we had a major spill. That's when I started bird rescue and set this place up."

She opened an old refrigerator in the corner and took out a bag of smelly fish. She handed the bag to Joe. "Now, how about you feeding these hungry birds while Jason and I start washing this one?"

Melanie half filled both basins of the double sink with warm water, and Jason passed the tern to her. She cautiously unwrapped it, avoiding its sharp beak, and put it in the left side.

"Now, Jason, you hold it while I wash."

She squirted detergent onto the tern's feathers and gently worked it in all over. When the water was dirty, she washed the bird again in clean water. She did this several times until the bird was clean.

When she was satisfied that no oil was left on the tern's feathers, she gave it a final rinse. "We have to get every bit of soap out," she said. "Before we let the birds go, I have to try them out in a pool. If there is any soap left on them, they can't float."

"What can we do to help the other birds out there?" asked Joe.

"Well," said Melanie, "whenever you're on the beach, you could look out for oil and bring in any birds that are caught in it. That would help a lot because I'm too busy here to get outside every day."

"We can do that," said Jason. "If we get a bunch of kids together to help, we can set up a schedule so we can cover the whole beach every day. We can be the Winter Beach Patrol! Joe and I'll walk the beach tomorrow after school, and then we'll be back to see you to find out how our tern is doing."

"That's great," said Melanie. "The more birds we find before they get too much oil inside them, the more birds we can save. Together, the Winter Beach Patrol and this center are going to make a great team!"